Whitney HOUSTON

GRADY LIBRARY

Whitney HOUSTON

Keith Elliot Greenberg

Lerner Publications Company
Minneapolis

Acknowledgments

The author wishes to thank Mike Liben and the staff of *Teen Beat* magazine for opening their files to him for the research of this book. Information was derived from *Time*, *Us*, *Jet*, and *Ebony* magazines as well as other publications.

Manufactured in the United States of America

LIBRARY OF CONGRESS CATALOGING-IN-PUBLICATION DATA

Greenberg, Keith Elliot.
  Whitney Houston / Keith Elliot Greenberg.
    p.   cm.
    Summary: Traces the life and career of the popular black singer who has been called the "prom queen of soul."
  ISBN 0-8225-1619-5 (lib. bdg.)
    1. Houston, Whitney—Juvenile literature. 2. Singers—United States—Biography—Juvenile literature. [1. Houston, Whitney. 2. Singers. 3. Afro-Americans—Biography.] I. Title.
ML3930.H7G7   1988
784.5′0092′4—dc19
[B]
[92]   87-36062
                                                                        CIP
                                                                     MN AC

3   4   5   6   7   8   9   10   98   97   96   95   94   93   92   91

Contents

She's Got It

Arista Records president Clive Davis summed up Whitney Houston's sensational talents in two sentences shortly after she decided to make music for his company. The two appeared on "The Merv Griffin Show" and Davis explained to the television audience the reason he considered the pretty young singer a star of the future. "You either got it or you don't," he said. "She's got it."

It wasn't long before his words rang true to the world. From the moment Whitney Houston's songs hit the radio, it seemed that everybody was in love with the

Whitney succeeds with a dynamite combination of good looks, glamour, and a great voice.

performer. Her first album, *Whitney Houston*, sold more than 14 million copies worldwide, making it the best-selling debut album ever and the most popular collection by a black female.

The ex-model's beauty, politeness, and dedication to her art only added to her fame. *Time* magazine called her "the prom queen of soul," stating that "everybody around wants to adopt her, escort her or be her."

At every music awards ceremony, Whitney's name is on attendees' minds and lips. Having won the top honors of the recording business—two Grammy awards and several American Music Awards—Whitney has achieved in a few years what most entertainers spend lifetimes dreaming about.

Unlike celebrities who show off success with flashy cars and loud jewelry, Whitney has remained private and modest. She gains satisfaction through her creativity, family, and friendships.

She vows not to change her humble personality. "Success hasn't changed me the way it can change some people," she says. "My family helps me to maintain a good head, and to try to keep everything in balance."

Deeply religious, Whitney openly thanks God for her good fortune. "I'm blessed," she states, "blessed with this voice, which was just given to me, and blessed with people who love me and care about me."

She wants fans to know that the person they see on stage is Whitney Houston as she really is—without insincere gimmicks: "God gave me a voice to sing with, and when you have that, what other gimmick is there?"

Starting Out

Whitney Houston was born on August 9, 1963, to a musical, church-going family in Newark, New Jersey. She is the youngest of three children. Newark, located close to New York City, had long been home to many ethnic groups working hard to enjoy a piece of the American dream. By the time Whitney was growing up, however, poverty and crime had forced many residents to flee Newark. The Houstons' strong family ties and

Cissy Houston (left) taught Whitney to sing.

the lessons Whitney learned at Newark's New Hope Baptist Church helped keep the youngster out of trouble.

In 1967, Newark exploded into riots. Angry blacks protested the difficult living conditions and racial discrimination they faced. Terrified, Whitney and her brothers huddled in their home while looting, fights, and fires raged outside. When the violence ended, Whitney's parents decided to move the children to a safer environment. The family relocated to a two-story house in suburban East Orange, New Jersey.

Even after the Houstons moved, they stayed involved with New Hope Baptist Church, where Whitney's mother, Cissy, was choir director. Cissy had begun singing as a child member of the Drinkard Singers, a gospel group. As she grew, so did her musical abilities. She was founder and lead singer of the soul group Sweet Inspirations—creators of the Top Twenty hit "Sweet Inspiration" in 1968. Cissy was the first person to record "Midnight Train to Georgia," later a hit for Gladys Knight and the Pips. Stars like Aretha Franklin and the late Elvis Presley also sought out Cissy's high-ranging voice for background vocals.

Whitney's father, John— who later became executive secretary of Newark's Central Planning Board—was Cissy's manager and head of the household during the long periods his wife spent touring. Whitney remembers, "He was Mom's support network while she was on

12

tour. He changed diapers, cooked, did my hair and dressed me, all the while providing Mom with advice and answers."

No matter how busy they were, Whitney's parents made time to listen to their children's questions and steer them in a positive direction. Cissy has said that her child-rearing philosophy is expressed in Whitney's hit song, "Greatest Love": *I believe the children are our future, teach them well and let them lead the way.*

Between Cissy's musical gifts and John's knowledge of the entertainment industry, the Houston children were well prepared to become leaders in the performing field. Both of Whitney's older brothers play important roles in her act. Michael is production manager when she tours. Half-brother Gary Garland sings duets with her, as well as backup vocals.

Other influences on Whitney when she was growing up were her cousin Dionne Warwick, a 1960s music wonder who still plays to packed houses, and Cissy's friend Aretha Franklin, who was the first woman voted into the Rock and Roll Hall of Fame. In the Houston home, Aretha was called Aunt Ree.

Dionne says that she always knew that great things were in store for Whitney, whom Dionne thinks of as the little girl she never had. Warwick believes that Whitney's talent and good looks gave her just the right credentials to become successful.

Whitney sang a solo on stage for the first time at the New Hope Baptist Church in Newark.

Yet the child received no special favors from Cissy, a strict mother who insisted that Whitney conduct herself politely and with consideration for others. John says Cissy taught the girl how to talk well, walk, stand up straight, and greet people.

Cissy recalls, "I didn't need anyone to enforce my rules. Early dating, cruising around—she wasn't going to do that.... She wasn't going to wear stockings until I said okay, even if her friends did. No makeup, no lipstick, no high heels. And no discussion.

"She didn't like it. She hated it. Sometimes she

14

would go to her father—her brothers would too—because they thought he was a little more lenient. But they didn't get around what I told them."

While other kids pretended to be nurses and fire-fighters, Whitney made believe she was a radio queen. Her brother Gary reminisces that she would dress up in Cissy's clothes and pretend she was singing in Madison Square Garden.

"I remember when I was about 12, I would go into our basement where my mother had her recording equipment," Whitney says. "I'd take the microphone, put on Aretha Franklin's music and go at it for hours, closing my eyes and singing all by myself. I imagined I was on stage singing to a packed house."

At the age of 11, Whitney sang a solo on a stage for the first time. The event: a church show. The song: "Guide Me, O Thou Great Jehovah." She says, "I was scared to death. I was aware of people staring at me. No one moved. They seemed almost in a trance. I just stared at the clock in the center of the church. When I finished, everyone clapped and started crying."

There would be similar reactions every time Whitney performed afterward. What had been obvious to Cissy Houston, Aretha Franklin, and Dionne Warwick was now clear to the child. About a year after her debut on the church stage, Whitney decided to follow in her mother's footsteps as a professional.

15

Growing

Finding a singing teacher was the easiest task Whitney ever had. Cissy Houston agreed to take her daughter on the road and include the youngster in her act.

"My mom taught me everything that I know about this business, about singing, studio work and things like that," Whitney says.

At first, the girl sang backup vocals for her mother. Slowly, Cissy brought her daughter into the spotlight. "I had a song to do and then as I got a little older, she gave me two songs to do and I went on from there," Whitney says.

With each performance came a new lesson. Cissy taught her not to start loud because she would have to get louder. She told Whitney that songs tell a story—and proper pronunciation is the best way for the musical story to be understood.

Although she was a Baptist, Whitney was sent to an all-girls Catholic high school, because Cissy approved of the discipline and level of education. It was during her high school years that the young singer had to endure one of the most difficult trials of her life—her parents' separation. Whitney says she learned about love and sacrifice from the experience. Her parents realized that the only way for them to stay together was to be apart for awhile.

Whitney transferred the heartfelt emotion triggered by her parents' breakup to her singing—and the audience —during her moving performances. Concert offers piled up. As Whitney received stage exposure, spectators were struck by her beauty as well as her voice. Modeling and television assignments followed. While continuing to sing alongside her mother, Whitney appeared in magazines like *Glamour*, *Seventeen*, *Young Miss*, and *Cosmopolitan* and acted on the television programs "Silver Spoons" and "Gimme a Break."

Never did she become sidetracked from her main goal, though. "I like modeling," Whitney says. "But singing was in my blood. There was no way to escape that."

Arista Records president Clive Davis was not about to allow the singer to escape from him. In 1983, the man who helped launch the careers of Janis Joplin, Billy Joel, and Barry Manilow signed Whitney to his recording label. So valuable was she to Davis that he inserted a special condition into the contract—if he leaves Arista, Whitney can leave with him.

Like her mother, Whitney began singing backup vocals on other performers' albums. She worked with Lou Rawls, Paul Jabara, Chaka Khan, and The Neville Brothers.

But Whitney's talents were too great to restrict to other entertainers' records. Her music internship complete, the young woman was ready to strike out on her own!

Bursting Forth

Realizing Whitney's tremendous value to Arista Records, Clive Davis and his assistants were extra careful when planning her first album. Before choosing a song, they asked, "Will it be a hit?" The cautious team took two years to pick the right tunes.

Old friends Teddy Pendergrass and Jermaine Jackson helped out. Whitney performed "Hold Me" with Pendergrass and "Take Good Care of My Heart" with Jackson. She and Jermaine also sang and acted together on the daytime drama "As The World Turns" when the record was released.

Three of the top producers in the music business were called in: Kashif, known for his work with singer George Benson; Michael Masser, credited with assisting Pendergrass and Diana Ross; and Narada Michael Walden, distinguished for creating hits for performers like Angela Bofill and Stephanie Mills.

The record, *Whitney Houston*, was released on Valentine's Day, 1985—the perfect date for the premiere of America's latest sweetheart. The album shot to the top of the music charts, outselling collections by such stars as Cyndi Lauper, David Lee Roth, Run-D.M.C., Billy Joel, and former Beatle Paul McCartney.

Newspaper and magazine reviewers, generally feared by entertainers because of their biting criticism, could not praise Whitney enough. The *New York Times* called her "a talent with tremendous potential." The weekly *Village Voice* newspaper said, "She has a big voice, the kind that makes you laugh and weep at the same time." In her hometown of Newark, New Jersey, the *Star-Ledger* raved, "There is no doubt about it, Whitney Houston is going to be a star."

Fame always brings countless new "friends" eager to enjoy the benefits of knowing a celebrity. But Whitney stuck with family and close friends. She went on her first tour surrounded by family members, and she placed her business interests in the trustworthy hands of her father, John.

Whitney says of her mother, Cissy Houston: "She's my teacher, my adviser—my greatest inspiration."

Her daughter's popularity renewed interest in Cissy's career. "It has helped me a great deal," Cissy says. "More and more people call every day. I really wanted to slow down but I'm getting just as busy.

"People are now realizing that she's my daughter and that I taught her and she worked with me in clubs and concerts."

A special moment between mother and daughter occurred during the making of the "Greatest Love" video. Cissy appeared in the production, urging Whitney to believe in herself. Whitney gave her mother a thankful—and very genuine—hug.

Superstar

Music fans anxiously awaited Whitney's second album. Many wondered if the record could be as good as the first. The release would prove whether Whitney was a true superstar or simply a passing marvel.

Whitney tried not to let the pressure bother her. "I'm going in there and doing it just like the first one with everything I've got and try to make it the best it can possibly be," she explained. "As far as the public is concerned, it depends on them."

Narada Michael Walden, Michael Masser, and Kashif returned to help with the second album. A newcomer to the project was John "Jellybean" Benitez, who was partly responsible for launching the career of Madonna. Benitez produced "Love Will Save The Day."

Houston's second album, *Whitney*—a summer 1987 favorite—broke new records. It was the first collection by a female to start at Number One on *Billboard* magazine's pop music chart. The song "I Wanna Dance With Somebody (Who Loves Me)" shot to the top of eight different *Billboard* hit lists.

Although some critics thought *Whitney*'s sound was too controlled, the album was a commercial success, pleasing the singer's many fans. A reviewer in *Rolling Stone* magazine said, "After several listens, it's nearly impossible to dislodge Whitney from your brain."

With her third album, released in late 1990, Whitney again proved herself to both critics and fans. While the title track became a best-selling single and a video hit, many reviewers called *I'm Your Baby Tonight* Whitney's best album.

The former model impressed video viewers with what *Glamour* magazine called "drop dead" good looks. Whitney says she loves the camera—and it loves her. Her ease in front of the camera helped her create dynamic music videos. She says that videos allow her "to see how the visual and the music work together."

Whitney's success paved the way for other blacks and women to gain recognition in the music business. "Here

Whitney has received several American Music Awards—a good reason to smile.

I come with the right skin, the right voice, the right style, the right everything...and VOOM! it's a little easier for the others," she explains.

Grateful

Outside the studio and away from the stage, Whitney describes her life as "ordinary": "I really do very ordinary things...I eat, sleep, sing, play tennis, play with my cats. Being alone is very important to me, but when I'm with friends I laugh, joke, fool around. Act normal."

Whitney prefers a quiet lifestyle and says she doesn't like to go out to nightclubs. She also avoids drugs. "I just don't want drugs to be a part of my life," she says, "because I know eventually they will ruin you. Drugs kill you mentally and physically. You'll die one way or another."

Dionne Warwick and Cissy Houston were the two most important influences on Whitney's music.

Some of Whitney's most creative moments happen in the quiet of the large western New Jersey home she bought with the profits from her record sales. She has learned that being famous sometimes means keeping a safe distance from admirers who can innocently overwhelm an entertainer with affection. Being alone does not necessarily mean being lonesome, though, Whitney says. "When I decided to be a singer, my mother warned me I'd be alone a lot. Basically, we all are. Loneliness comes with life."

Cissy believes that her daughter will one day have a family: "It's just a matter of finding the right time and the right person. She's got to find someone who loves her for herself, not for her money or anything."

First, though, Whitney hopes to record a gospel album. The entertainer has been singing gospel tunes and hymns since she was a child, and she includes melodies about the Bible in her stage show. "It's part of me," Whitney says. "It's part of my voice and part of my life. Someday I would like to do a gospel album and record with my mother and Dionne."

Not a day passes when Whitney does not thank God for her skills and accomplishments. "I'm just so grateful and I'm so thankful to Him for what He's given me," she says. "So many things can happen to one who is successful, so that you can just get taken away. But the Father has kept me level. I know I can't get any bigger than Him."

Whitney's father, John Houston, acts as her business manager.

Photo credits:

Todd Kaplan/Star File, pp. 1, 20, 28
Ross Marino/London Features International, p. 2
Chris V.D. Vooren/Retna Ltd., p. 6
Michael Putland/Retna Ltd., p. 8
The Star Ledger, p. 10
Courtesy of New Hope Baptist Church, p. 14
M. Harlan/Star File, p. 16
Vinnie Zuffante/Star File, pp. 23, 24
Chris Walter/Retna Ltd., p. 27
Ralph Dominguez/Globe Photos, p. 30
Scott Weiner/Retna Ltd., p. 32

Front and back cover photos by Barry Talesnick/Retna Ltd.